This book belongs to

••••••••••••••••••••••••••••••••••••

••••••••••••••••••••••••••••••••••••

For Tony Lawson,
a keen and practical grandad
I.W.

For Charlie, Izzie and Alfie
and Sarah Malley, superstar
S.M.

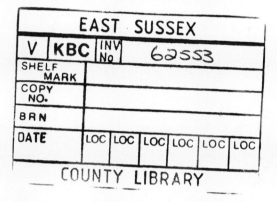

First published in 2003 in Great Britain by Gullane Children's Books
This paperback edition published in 2003 by

GULLANE
CHILDREN'S BOOKS

Winchester House, 259-269 Old Marylebone Road,
London NW1 5XJ

3 5 7 9 10 8 6 4 2

Text © Ian Whybrow 2003
Illustrations © Sarah Massini 2003

The right of Ian Whybrow and Sarah Massini to be identified as the author and illustrator of this work
has been asserted by them in accordance with the Copyright, Designs, and Patents Act, 1988.
A CIP record for this title is available from the British Library.

ISBN 1-86233-332-7 hardback
ISBN 1-86233-495-1 paperback

Printed and bound in China

I'd Rather Go To Grandad's

IAN WHYBROW ☼ SARAH MASSINI

GULLANE
CHILDREN'S BOOKS

Grandad is coming to fetch me.
Here he comes at last!
I'm going to stay at his house today,
That's why I'm running so fast!

Bus Stop

I like going to theme parks,
And I like going to the zoo.
But best of all I like Grandad's house,
And that's where we're going to.

First we go on a big fast bus,
Then we go on a train.
And I can hold the tickets
For there and back again.

I like going on aeroplanes,
I like big ships on the sea,
But best of all I love Grandad's boat
And that's where I'd rather be.

Grandad lives in a lighthouse
And we row to get across,
Some people think that's very hard,
But it isn't hard for us!

Grandad's house is very tall.
It guides the ships in the night.
And you have to climb a hundred steps
To reach the shining light!

We don't bother to watch TV
Or look at videos.
Grandad and I like making things;
We've made a kart that goes!

When you sit in Grandad's kitchen
It's like being in the sky!
You can look right down on a tiny town,
Like the seagulls that glide by.

He has a garden made of sand.
Sometimes we make a fire.
We cook our supper and warm our toes
While the sparks go higher and higher.

I like Mum and Dad's big bed,
And I like my bed (which is small),
But I've got a hammock at Grandad's house
And I like that best of all.